Lance's Story

By Cala Spinner

Illustrated by Patrick Spaziante

Ready-to-Read

Simon Spotlight

New York London Toronto Sydney New Delhi

SIMON SPOTLIGHT

An imprint of Simon & Schuster Children's Publishing Division
1230 Avenue of the Americas, New York, New York 10020
This Simon Spotlight edition August 2018

For information about
special discounts for bulk purchases, please contact Simon & Schuster Special Sales at
1-866-506-1949 or business@simonandschuster.com.
Manufactured in the United States of America 0718 LAK
2 4 6 8 10 9 7 5 3 1
ISBN 978-1-5344-2540-8 (hc)
ISBN 978-1-5344-2539-2 (pbk)
ISBN 978-1-5344-2541-5 (eBook)

Hey there! My name is Lance.
You probably know that already.
I'm kind of a big deal.

On Earth, I was the best pilot
at the Galaxy Garrison,
a school for pilots.
Some people thought
another pilot named Keith was
the best, but nope, it was me.
I am called "The Tailor" because of
how I threaded the needle.

That meant I flew near my target.
My friend Hunk didn't like
threading the needle.
He threw up a lot.
It's Hunk's fault—and not mine—
that we failed our flight tests.

I have a big family.
There are my brothers,
Luis and Marco,
and my sisters,
Veronica and Rachel.
I am the youngest.

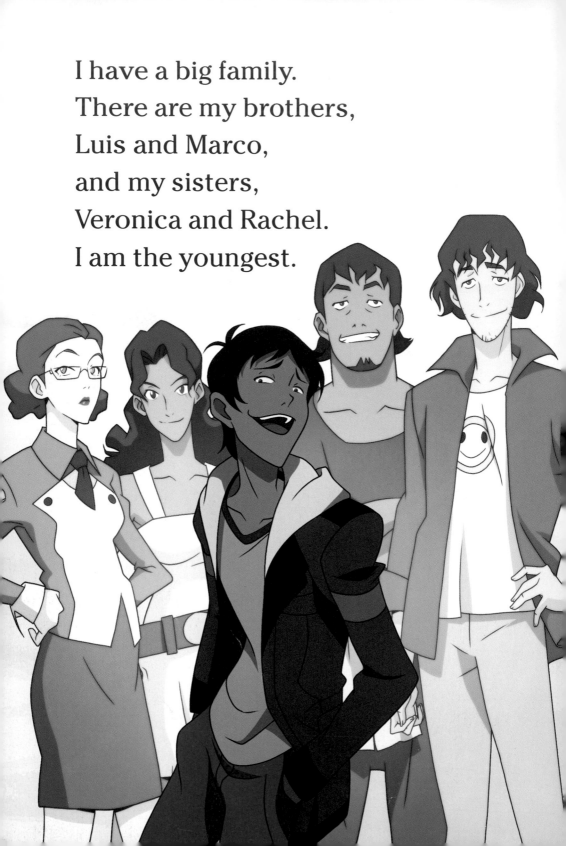

I have a niece, a nephew,
parents, and grandparents, too.
I miss them all.
I also miss Varadero Beach
and eating garlic knots.

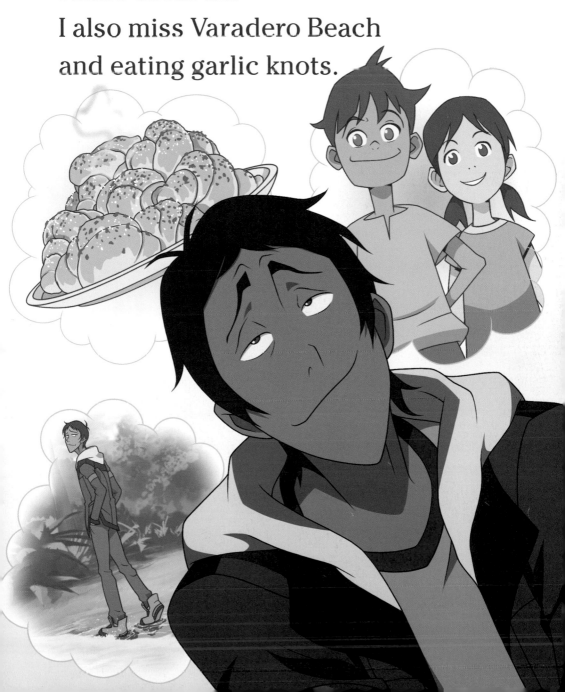

I wish I could visit my family,
but I have important work to do.
See, I'm not just
a boy from Cuba.

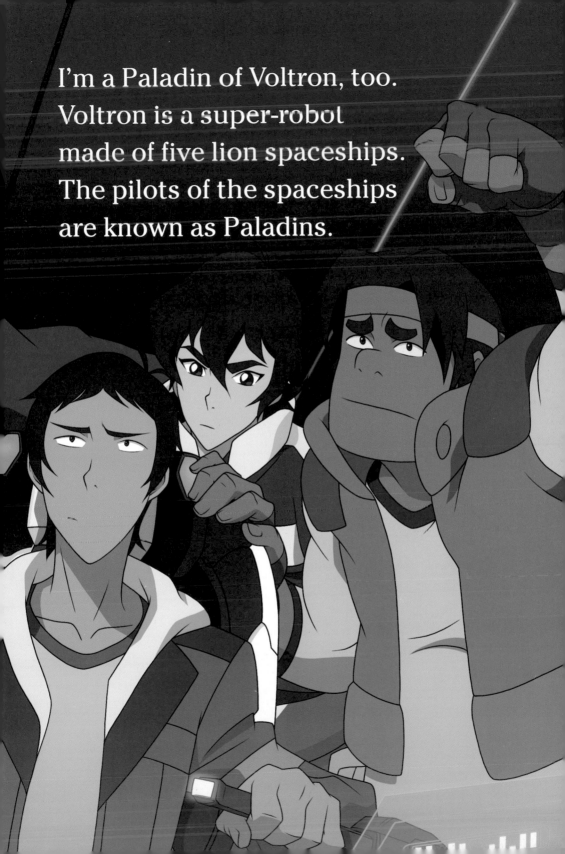

I'm a Paladin of Voltron, too. Voltron is a super-robot made of five lion spaceships. The pilots of the spaceships are known as Paladins.

That means I help protect
the universe while piloting
my spaceship.
At first, I flew the Blue Lion.
Blue and I were tight.

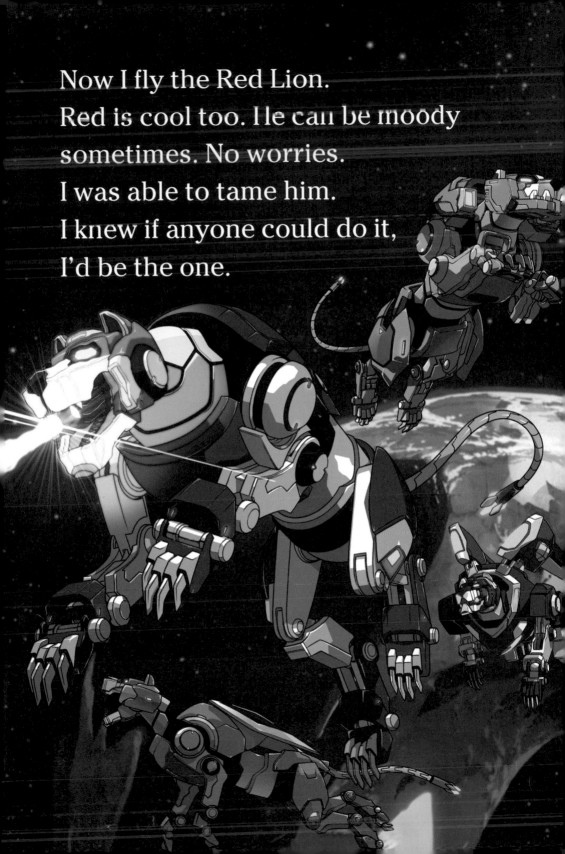

Now I fly the Red Lion.
Red is cool too. He can be moody
sometimes. No worries.
I was able to tame him.
I knew if anyone could do it,
I'd be the one.

I like being part of the team.
I also like going to the pool
when I'm not protecting
the universe.

What I mean to say is,
I like going to the pool *alone*.
I don't like to share it,
especially not with Keith.

There are lots of cool things about being a Paladin— aside from getting to fly around and defend the universe.

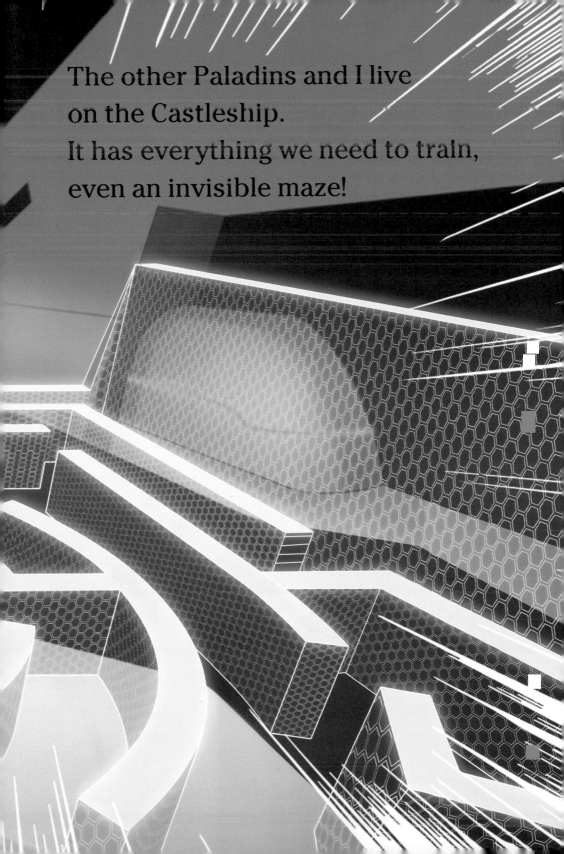

The other Paladins and I live on the Castleship. It has everything we need to train, even an invisible maze!

I take care of Kaltenecker.
What is Kaltenecker, you ask?
Kaltenecker is our cow.

We had no way
to make milkshakes
until we got Kaltenecker!

I also get to meet aliens from
different planets! Princess Allura
was the first alien I met.
She is from the planet Altea.
She was our guide,
but now she is a Paladin.
I like Allura a lot.
Don't tell her, okay?

I even have special lion slippers.

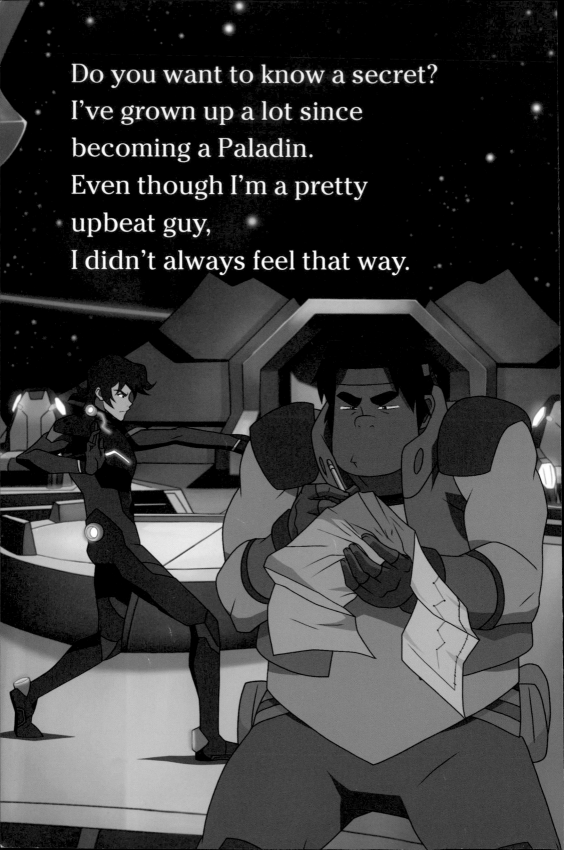

Do you want to know a secret?
I've grown up a lot since
becoming a Paladin.
Even though I'm a pretty
upbeat guy,
I didn't always feel that way.

Everyone had a role.
Shiro was the leader.
Pidge was the coder.
Hunk was the engineer.
Keith was the fighter.

I didn't know what my role was.
I felt like a fifth wheel—
or seventh, if you count
Allura and our advisor, Coran.

But once I accepted Keith
as the new leader of Voltron,
something amazing happened.
I took over the Red Lion and
became Voltron's right-arm man.

I've learned that teamwork is important, especially in outer space.

And you know what?
Maybe someday I *will* share
the pool, even with Keith.
His mullet isn't so bad after all.

I am going to return
to Earth one day.

First I'll hug my mom.
Then I'll eat garlic knots from
my favorite place at the beach.

After that, I'll find Pidge. Maybe I'll bring peanut butter cookies.

We can play the video game
that we bought
at the space mall.

I need to defeat
the Galra Empire
before I return home.

I am a Paladin.
The team needs me.

And the universe needs Voltron.
I told you
I'm a big deal,
didn't I?

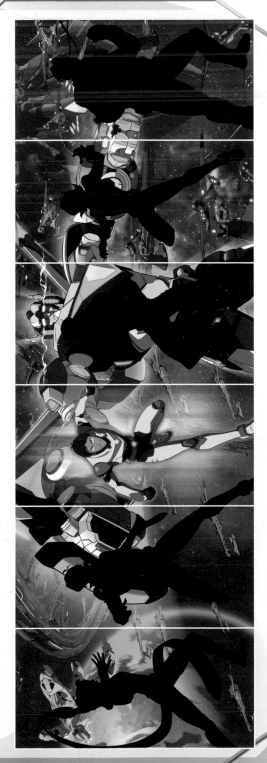

COLLECT ALL SIX POSTERS TO FORM VOLTRON!

LANCE

A class clown and the most eager to prove himself, Lance is bonded to the Blue Lion.

STATS

- **Nickname:** The Tailor (because he can thread the needle)
- **Birthday:** July 28
- **Heritage:** Cuban
- **Age:** 17

STRENGTH //////////////////////
AGILITY //////////////////////
INTELLIGENCE //////////////////////

BLUE LION
Guardian Spirit of the Water

Voltron Position: right leg
Found: Earth

CAPABILITIES

- **Tail Laser:** moderately damages targets at long range
- **Mouth Cannon:** severely damages targets at long range
- **Jaw Blade:** cuts through targets at very close range
- **Ice Ray:** freezes long-range targets on contact
- **Hidden Power:** Sonic Cannon, used to repel enemies and echolocate

DAMAGE //////////////////////
ARMOR //////////////////////
SPEED //////////////////////